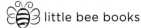 little bee books

New York, NY
Text copyright © 2022 by Cort Lane
Illustrations copyright © 2022 by Little Bee Books
All rights reserved, including the right of reproduction
in whole or in part in any form.
Library of Congress Cataloging-in-Publication Data
is available upon request.
For information about special discounts on bulk purchases,
please contact Little Bee Books at sales@littlebeebooks.com.
Manufactured in China   RRD 0322
ISBN 978-1-4998-1295-4 (paperback)
First Edition 10 9 8 7 6 5 4 3 2 1
ISBN 978-1-4998-1296-1 (hardcover)
First Edition 10 9 8 7 6 5 4 3 2 1
ISBN 978-1-4998-1297-8 (ebook)

littlebeebooks.com

MONSTER AND ME

THE PALACE PRANKSTER

BY CORT LANE

ILLUSTRATED BY ANKITHA KINI

little bee books

Contents

Chapter 1:
Orange You Glad You Came To the Festival?

Freddy von Frankenstein was on a secret mission. He lived high up in the Himalaya Mountains, in a country called Nepal. Today he snuck into the town at the foot of the mountains with a giddy smile. The townspeople were celebrating the most exciting event in Nepal . . . the Biska Jatra festival!

All the townspeople were celebrating the new year with music and dancing. But Freddy thought the most fun part was that they flung a bright, red-orange powder called "sindoor" at each other. Everyone was covered in orange! This special day, called Sindoor Jatra, is celebrated like this every year.

Freddy had watched the festival from the top of the mountain for years. And this time, he was determined to join the fun. Freddy shouted, "Time to get splattered!" as he ran into the crowd to get covered in sindoor. But just then, he heard the sound of *Bzzzt bzzzt!* He was getting a surprise video call on his wrist communicator.

"Bummer," moaned Freddy. He wanted to ignore it and continue celebrating, but the call was from his brother and best friend, F.M., so he answered.

"Where are you?!" his big brother asked.

"I'm down in the village about to get covered head to toe in orange stuff!" said Freddy.

F.M. looked worried. "Freddy, you're not supposed to go down to the village alone. You're gonna get in trouble!"

Freddy laughed and said, "Come down and join in, and then I won't be alone. And you can have a good time getting splattered too! Pleeeease. You don't want me to get into trouble, do you?"

Freddy was usually pretty good at convincing F.M. to go along with his schemes. But not this time! Hanging out in a crowd of humans was just about the scariest thing F.M. could imagine. When he was created by Freddy's dad, Victor, the local villagers were terrified. They chased Victor and F.M. out of town, and F.M. has been afraid of people ever since.

So F.M. quickly changed the subject. "But Mom is looking for you! You're behind on your chores,

so you'd better zoom back up to the palace before she learns you've snuck out. Riya and I are already half-done with ours!"

Freddy groaned with disappointment. Having a brother and sister who always did the right thing was no fun. He hopped on his super-cycle and raced up the mountain, using the turbo boost to make it back in record time.

Chapter 2:
Caught Orange-Handed

Freddy walked into the kitchen and saw Mom, F.M., his adopted sister, Riya, and their pet monkey, Igor, eating their lunches. His mother, Shan, asked, "Where have you been all morning, Freddy?!"

Victor, his dad, was there too. But he was so distracted fiddling with some tech that he hadn't even touched his lunch. Freddy's dad was the famous scientist, Victor Von Frankenstein.

"Hey, what's the new invention Dad?" asked Freddy, trying to avoid telling his parents where he had been.

"It's a controller for my flotation bubbles!" Victor answered. "Without the controller operating them, the bubbles float anywhere willy-nilly. But the signal is messed up." Freddy slyly asked, "Can I help you, Dad?"

But Shan saw that Freddy was trying once again to avoid his responsibilities. She said, "No, you have all of your chores from the week saved up. And you need to get to all of them today—no more goofing off." Freddy turned to her to argue, but in doing so, Shan noticed a *big* spot of orange powder on the other side of his face.

"Were you in town for the Biska Jatra festival?!" she shouted.

Uh-oh, thought Freddy. His mom rarely lost her cool. But now she was furious to see that Freddy disobeyed and went down on his own.

"Everybody in this house has responsibilities to our family," scolded Shan. "And you need to learn to stop acting selfish. Go clean your messy room, and then come back down and finish your other chores."

Freddy was wide-eyed with shock. "But that's gonna take all day!" he protested. *And I like my room messy, with tech parts and wires and half-done inventions everywhere*, he thought. *I know where everything is!*

His mom angrily pointed to the stairs. Freddy pouted and shuffled off to clean his room.

Chapter 3:
Pop Goes the Bubble!

F.M. and Riya walked into Freddy's room, trying to cheer him up.

Riya asked, "Why don't you like cleaning your room?"

Ugh, thought Freddy, *who likes cleaning?*

Riya continued, "I love my new room. I take pride in keeping it tidy and pretty!" Freddy took his room for granted, but Riya was so excited to have a space of her own.

As Freddy rolled his eyes at Riya, there was a loud popping noise that startled all three of them.

POP! POP! POP!

It seemed to be coming from the lab downstairs. Then they heard mom and dad yelling, so they all quickly ran down to the lab. F.M. nearly fell down the stairs with fright. There they saw both Victor and Shan, covered in orange goo!

Dad's bubble invention must have gone horribly wrong! thought Freddy. *This is a disaster . . . but it's also a little funny too.*

Freddy heard a giggle and looked around to see who it was, but it didn't sound like F.M. or Riya. Victor turned to Freddy and asked, "Do you think this is funny? Because it is definitely NOT!"

"That giggling wasn't me, I swear!" said Freddy, as he stifled a laugh himself.

Victor sighed and said, "Kids, we need you to help clean the goo off the lab."

"What?! Why us? We didn't make the mess!" protested Freddy.

Shan answered skeptically, "Even if you didn't, we really need help cleaning it."

"No way!" Freddy was frustrated. *Punished for something I didn't even do!*

After Mom and Dad left to wash the goo off themselves, Freddy complained, "I can't believe I left the festival just to be punished all day."

Riya's eyes lit up. "You went to the festival? Oh, please tell me all about it!" she asked Freddy. "Dancing and music and orange powder, it sounds like so much fun!"

"Maybe later," Freddy said with a pout. "I have too many chores to do now."

"We'll help out. We know you didn't do this," F.M. said, relieved to have chores to keep them away from the crowd in the town below.

They tried to sweep up the orange goo with brooms, but it just pushed the mess around.

"I think we need some mops," Freddy said, wiping his brow.

Riya nodded. "Agreed, this doesn't seem to be working." As they went to find some, suddenly, an explosion shook the palace.

KAPOW!

"What's happening now?!" F.M. moaned.

"That sounded like it came from the kitchen!" Riya said.

They raced down, and arrived at quite a sight— the pineapple buns Shan had just baked had exploded like snow all over her kitchen. Little bread flakes were still floating down.

"Two disasters in a row. Are we being pranked?" F.M. wondered.

Riya asked, "What is pranked?"

"Pranks are naughty tricks some people do to make mischief," Shan explained. "Maybe somebody is busy doing pranks because they are too bored doing their chores." She looked sternly right at Freddy as she said it.

Freddy was shocked! "Hey, I had nothing to do with either explosion! And they're only making more chores for me!"

Now I'm getting blamed for this too? thought Freddy. *I'll show Mom that she's wrong.* "I'm going to find out who this prankster is. I'll investigate, like a detective!"

"I think you probably just want to do something more fun than chores." F.M. teased.

But Freddy was in no mood. *Not even my brother is taking my side?!* He stormed off to his room.

Chapter 4:
Detective Freddy Is on the Case

"**I**'ll get to the bottom of this!" Freddy vowed as he packed high-tech detective inventions in his backpack to help him investigate. *As Inspector Freddy Von Frankenstein does, I'll use my smarts to expose the prankster.*

Freddy first went to check Victor's security system and saw that no one else had entered the front door all day. *So it has to be someone in the house. Hmmm, only Dad, Mom, F.M., Riya, and Igor live in the palace*, he thought.

Next, Freddy sorted through the suspects. *Dad and Mom were furious about the pranks, so it couldn't be them. F.M. is too afraid of explosions and loud noises, so it couldn't be him either! That leaves Riya and Igor as my only suspects.* Freddy was pleased that he was off to a good start.

But a great detective needs a great sidekick, thought Freddy. *I'll enlist F.M. as my assistant detective.* Finding F.M. alone in the lab mopping up goo, he pleaded, "You gotta help me figure out who's behind the pranks!"

"OK," F.M. replied, "but just because I don't like to see Mom mad at you."

Freddy shared his evidence. "It could be Igor, but I think it's got to be Riya. We only met her a few weeks ago. What do we *really* know about her?"

"Well, she didn't even know what a prank is." F.M. pointed out. "And don't you remember, she used her werecat powers to help us stop the Yeti. It can't be her!"

Even though Freddy thought this was pretty convincing, he still dragged F.M. to the kitchen to interrogate Riya. She was busy cleaning up the kitchen mess.

"You were the one who caused the explosions today, admit it!" accused Freddy. Riya looked shocked, and then hurt.

"How could you say that?!" she asked.

Freddy almost felt a touch of guilt, but all of a sudden a big wet noise came from upstairs.

SPLAT!

Another explosion?!? They looked at each other, then all three of them ran up to find Riya's newly decorated bedroom ruined with splattered purple paint everywhere.

Riya sank to her knees, "My . . . my room." She started to cry.

F.M. gave her a gentle hug and said, "We will make it nice again, I promise."

Freddy also felt sorry for her. *She can't be the prankster if her own room was ruined.*

"I'll figure out who did this!" Freddy swore to her. "I promise, Riya." He pulled on his high-tech goggles and scanned for clues. But his goggles couldn't spot any strange footprints.

Then Riya perked up and listened closely. "Did you hear that giggle?" asked Riya.

"Nope," both Freddy and F.M. said.

Riya remarked, "I think being a werecat means my senses are better, even when I'm in human form. I hear someone giggling far away."

"Wow, that's so cool!" said F.M., impressed with her ability.

Freddy tried to hide his envy. *I have to make my own tech to do that kind of stuff,* he thought.

"I think we really need Riya's super senses on our sleuth squad," F.M. insisted.

"Okay, just this once," sighed Freddy.

"So that leaves Igor as the last suspect," F.M. said. "Though I've never heard him giggle before. Can monkeys even do that?"

"He *does* really like to cause mischief," said Riya.

"Though he really only does so to get to food," added Detective Freddy. "Wait . . . food? Let's check the kitchen again!"

They ran back into the kitchen and found Igor—
but not sneaking food. He was trapped inside a
glass cookie jar! He banged furiously on the sides.

"Why would he be trapped in there? That
jar didn't even have cookies in it!" said F.M., who
always knew where the cookies were.

Hmmm, that's odd, thought Freddy. Freddy's face creased in worry. "Someone from outside *must* have snuck into the house to cause all this mischief!"

"But who could do that?" asked Riya.

Freddy was too busy pulling out a special scanning device to answer. He held the scanner up to the cookie jar to look for fingerprints. *Only Mom's fingerprints are on the cookie jar!* thought Freddy with surprise. Suddenly, he heard the same high-pitched laugh he heard when Shan's pineapple buns exploded blowing in through the window. They all stopped and looked at each other—all four of them could hear it that time!

Chapter 5:
A Haunted Palace?

Riya asked, "Does your scanner show anything?" Freddy shook his head. He was embarrassed that his detective smarts and cool tech hadn't been able to find anything yet. *No fingerprints. No footprints. Or any other clue*, he thought. *Some detective I am.*

"We know nobody walked into the house. So what kind of person could do this?" Freddy thought so hard his face turned red.

"What if it isn't a person at all?" wondered F.M. "What if it's a ghost? Could this old palace be . . . haunted?"

Freddy rolled his eyes at the idea. He refused to consider something like a ghost. But Riya agreed with F.M. "It's possible. After all, I'm a magical werecat—and we also met a Yeti!"

F.M. shouted, "There have to be more fantasticals out there!" Even Igor nodded in agreement.

The sleuth squad heard the distant giggling again. "We have to follow that giggle!" Riya shouted.

Freddy hesitated. Now this was starting to get creepy. *I have to be as brave as Riya*, he thought. *There must be a way my science smarts can figure this out!*

Freddy worked quickly to make a special new gadget. Pieces of wire and metal flew around wildly!

"Well, here's yet another mess to clean up!" F.M. joked. "Whatcha making, little brother?"

"It's a giggle-detector, obviously—to track the location of the laughs!" Freddie boasted. He turned it on and immediately, the device started beeping and pointing to the source of the giggles. And the arrow was pointing straight up!

A confused Riya asked, "Is it . . . pointing to the sky?" Wide-eyed, Freddy declared, "No—it's pointing to the attic!"

Freddy tried to act brave as he held his giggle gadget and climbed the stairs to the attic. Riya and Igor followed close behind, a little worried themselves. But no one was more scared than F.M., not so much because of the giggle but because he hated the attic. It was dark, creepy, and way high up—and F.M. was terribly afraid of heights. But just the same, he shakily crept up the tiny old stairs. After all, as a big brother, F.M. always protected his little brother and sister, no matter how scared he was.

As they climbed to the top of the stairs, the giggles got even louder. Freddy gulped and announced, "Here we are," as he opened the creaky door to the creepy attic. Freddy's device started to beep more quickly now.

"The attic is so big and dark I can't see how far it goes!" said Freddy. He could barely make out the old furniture, dust, and cobwebs.

"Let me take a look," said Riya. She bravely walked in first, using her special werecat eyesight and hearing to see what was there. Igor held onto her clothes and shivered as he walked with her.

F.M. warned, "No Riya, let me go first! I'm practically impossible to hurt." But suddenly, a metal door swung toward her.

"Watch out!" shouted Freddy. With cat-like reflexes, Riya jumped out of the way. But the door slammed into Igor as he shrieked. The door was attached to an ancient iron chest, and Igor was now trapped inside!

Igor howled with fear as F.M. ran to the chest. "I'll get you out, Igor!" But F.M. pulled and pulled with all his might on the door handle and it still wouldn't open.

"That's impossible!" said Freddy. "Your super-strength can open anything."

Riya looked worried. She turned to Freddy and said, "Unless magic is keeping it closed." "Magic?! There's no such thing," answered Freddy.

An annoyed Riya reminded him, "Well, when the moon comes out, MAGIC will turn me into a tiger-girl. Or did you forget about my werecat curse?"

"Hey, I have an idea," F.M. said. "My super-strength isn't from magic. It's from science. But maybe your supernatural tiger claws can fight the magic and free Igor."

"I hate to admit it, but he might be right," Freddy said. *IF the trap is really a magic one*, thought Freddy. "The sun will set pretty soon, so I think we will get to try out that theory when it does."

F.M. said to Igor, "We'll come back to get you, little buddy." But the monkey screeched with frustration anyway. They all crept forward to continue to search for the giggling prankster.

From the light of a tiny window, Riya could see a door on the other side of the attic. As they reached the wall, Freddy's gadget began to beep even more wildly. "It's pointing to the door," said Freddy.

"This time I'm going first," insisted F.M., even though his teeth were chattering with fear. Entering an even darker part of the attic was almost too much for him. The door was so little, F.M. could barely fit through. Freddy went in right behind.

WHAM!

The door slammed shut. Riya shouted, "Oh no! I'm trapped!"

F.M. fumbled in the dark and pulled on the handle. "And this door won't open either! This must be magic!" said F.M.

Freddy took in a deep breath and thought, *I can't explain any of this with science any more. None of my detective work or inventions are protecting us! Could it really be a ghost after all?* Riya shouted through the door, "Don't worry about me, I'll find a way to get over to you!"

Chapter 6:
Riya's Bravery

Riya thought about her new home, her new parents, and her new brothers. *I was so lonely and scared traveling across India before they took me in. I have to be brave right now and help them!*

Determined, Riya looked at the tiny window next to her. "I can probably climb around the edge of the roof and get to the other side of the attic!" she said to herself. "I wish the sun would hurry up and set, so the moon could turn me into a tiger-girl. Then the climbing would be easy. But there's no time to waste. Here I go!"

Riya pushed the window open and pulled herself out onto the roof. She was high up at the top of the palace's walls. "Don't look down, just keep going." As she slowly slid sideways along the roof, she could see another little window that would let her get back to the boys. "Almost there . . ." whispered Riya.

BOOM!

Something heavy fell on Riya, knocking her off the edge of the roof. "Noooooo!" she yelled. She started to fall, but didn't go far because the thing that fell on her was a net. She was trapped and dangling from the roof. First Igor and now her—this prankster was trapping them one by one!

Riya shouted, "Help! HEEEEEEELP!" Even down in the Palace, Victor and Shan could hear Riya yelling. They ran outside and were shocked to see her hanging from the top of the palace. "Oh no!" said Shan with worry. "We have to save her!"

"I'll find an invention to rescue her," Victor said. "You stay here and help keep her calm." Victor ran in. He was quite worried himself. "Could the boys be in danger too? I should have taken those pranks more seriously. Something strange is happening today!"

Victor entered the lab and said to himself, "If I can just get my flotation bubble controller working, I could float up to Riya and free her." He worked quickly to try to finish the controller. "Maybe I should have let Freddy help me earlier," said Victor.

Chapter 7:
An Escape Plan

Freddy was still up in the attic with F.M. They could hear Riya yelling for help. "What are we going to do?" moaned F.M.

We will probably be caught next, thought Freddy. We have to get out of here quick. *We are too easy to trap up here. My tech and detective skills have failed, so I have to think fast!*

Freddy's eyes lit up. He put on his high-tech goggles and looked right at the wall to his right. "What are you looking for?" asked F.M.

Freddy kept staring ahead and answered, "I'm scanning for an escape route. My goggles can see through the wall to the outside." Then Freddy touched part of the wall and shouted, "Punch through the wall right here!"

F.M. used his monster strength and easily punched through the wall. "But how will we get down from here?"

Freddy smiled as he looked outside and said, "We don't have to get down . . . yet. Look! Right there is the roof of the lab that slides open. And Dad can open it and get us down. We can call down to them for help and get out of this creepy old attic! I'm sure the prankster didn't plan on this surprise move!"

They climbed through the hole and carefully walked to the side of the lab roof. *Lucky that Dad is in his lab all the time*, thought Freddy.

"Dad! Mom! Help!" they shouted over and over. But nobody below responded.

F.M. groaned with fear from the height. "I don't like this at all, Freddy!" he complained.

Freddy was afraid too, but not from the height. "I'm afraid to go back in the attic and get trapped like Riya and Igor! Maybe I was wrong. Maybe ghosts are real. And very, VERY scary."

Freddy said, "Let's call out to them one more time. "Dad! Mom! Heeeeeelp!"

F.M. shouted as loud as he could with his big monster lungs, "HEEEEEEELP!" F.M.'s voice boomed through the mountains. F.M. couldn't even bear to look down, clinging to the roof. Suddenly, the roof panel over the lab started to slide open.

"Yeah!" cheered the brothers. Freddy shouted, "We're up here, Dad! Can you help us down?" F.M. sighed, "We're saved!"

But then . . . *Oh no*, Freddy thought. Loud giggles came from inside the lab. Freddy's giggle gadget started beeping wildly and pointing straight down. As Freddy nervously peered over the edge and down into the laboratory, one of Dad's orange-colored flotation bubbles rose quickly toward him. Freddy realized, *This is the final trap. This is how the ghost catches me! Mom and Dad aren't down there. They are probably trapped too. I'm doomed!* Paralyzed with fear, Freddy shut his eyes and prepared for his fate.

Then Freddy felt himself pulled to the side. Confused, he opened his eyes to see the bubble enveloping a terrified F.M. His brother had grabbed him to save him! But now F.M. was trapped.

Freddy scrunched his face and concentrated. *Think! Think! There has to be a way to save my brother from floating away*, thought Freddy.

F.M. was drifting farther and farther by the second. He was the most scared Freddy had ever seen him. And Freddy had seen his brother afraid nearly every day!

F.M. called out, "Don't worry about me! Just save our family by catching the person behind it all! You're smarter than me, Freddy, you're the only one who can do it!"

As Freddy sadly watched his big brother and best friend float away, he felt hopeless. *There's no telling what this ghost will do to my family next. But I still have to be brave, even if I'm just pretending*, he thought. *I'm the only one who isn't trapped.* Freddy's hands shook as he put his goggles back on and he walked slowly back to the hole in the attic.

He peered inside using his goggles. Their infrared vision showed someone moving around the attic. *Ghosts don't give off heat,* thought Freddy. *Hmmm. Maybe it's not a ghost after all!* Even though he was the most scared he'd ever been, Freddy climbed back into the attic. "Who are you? What do you want?" Freddy fearfully shouted.

All of a sudden, things started flying at Freddy—
first an old soccer ball bounced off him, then a dress
landed on him. Finally, a tuba fell on his head. This is
more silly than scary, he thought. *I'd laugh if I weren't
so mad!* Freddy pushed them all away and kept
moving forward. "I'll stop you yet, whatever you
are!" vowed Freddy.

Chapter 8:
The Chase Is On!

Meanwhile, F.M. was scared silly as his bubble floated away. After a while, the wind shifted, and it started to glide lower.

"Hooray!" shouted F.M. "If it lands on the ground, I can punch my way out and be free!" The monster was relieved until he saw where the wind was taking him . . . right into town . . . with thousands of people still at the Biska Jatra festival! "Everyone will see me. Oh no!"

Nothing scared F.M. more than a crowd of humans. He worried and watched as his bubble slowly floated down. "The sun is setting, so maybe they won't notice me in the dark," he wished. "Oh, this is the worst day EVER!"

***

Freddy was surprised that the door to the rest of the attic opened suddenly. His goggles could see that the creature was in that part of the attic. *Now is my chance to catch this thing*, thought Freddy.

Just as Freddy burst through the door, he heard a cackling, "Hee hee heeee!" It headed down the stairs on the far side.

Freddy gave chase. "Stop! You can't escape!" he yelled. He arrived at the top of the stairs and could see a shadow spiraling its way down.

It looks really small, thought Freddy. *And it's not running? It seems to be floating! Could it be a tiny fantastical?*

He zoomed down the stairs.

BOOM! BUMP!

Freddy looked back to see the giant iron chest that trapped Igor falling down the stairs behind him. "Oh no!" He could hear Igor screeching inside as it came bouncing down the stairs right at him. Freddy ran faster.

Below the fantastical squealed, "Hee! That'll getcha!"

I can't outrun the chest! thought Freddy. *I've got to use my smarts instead of my speed!* He concentrated really hard and calculated the timing and bounces of the chest. At just the right moment, he crouched low, and the chest went right over him and down the stairs. It bounced and crashed over and over.

With a final *SMASH* he heard an "Ooooof!"

At the bottom of the stairs he found a very odd little imp, dizzy from being hit by the chest. Igor, now free, took one look at it and ran away. As Freddy approached cautiously he thought, *I'll use my goggles to scan the villain.* His wrist communicator told him,

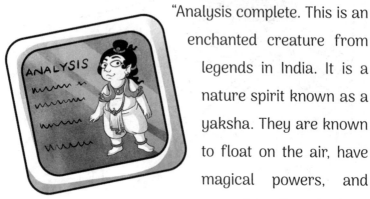

"Analysis complete. This is an enchanted creature from legends in India. It is a nature spirit known as a yaksha. They are known to float on the air, have magical powers, and cause lots of trouble."

The imp whined, "Hey, I don't cause trouble! I create fun! Especially when I'm bored."

Freddy cornered him and said, "You do cause trouble! You tricked my parents into thinking I was pulling all those pranks. Do you have a name, naughty yaksha?"

"I'm Uday," the imp giggled.

"Why are you here pranking us?" asked Freddy.

Uday pouted, "There's nothing yakshas hate more than being bored. I was *so* bored down in the jungle that I looked for a place to finally have some laughs. I could sense this place far away. I knew this mountain would be the perfect place for some fun. So I floated all the way up here!"

Hmm . . . Riya also came to this mountain because it drew her to it. And the Yeti was also drawn to the mountain, thought Freddy. *Three fantasticals in a row means some kind of magic energy attracts them.* But before Freddy could think any more about this new big mystery, Uday suddenly dazzled him with some colorful sparks.

Freddy covered his eyes. But the distraction allowed Uday to float away quickly, "Hee hee! Gotcha again, Freddy!"

Chapter 9:
The Final Trap

F.M. was covering his eyes too. He couldn't bear to see the people below him gathering to stare at the bubble. Surely they would be scared of his monstrous appearance and chase him.

As F.M. floated even closer to the town, he peered through his fingers. His bubble was headed right to the center of town. "No, no, no, NOOOOO!" he whimpered.

The sun was setting, and his big orange bubble reflected the sky. Villagers stopped dancing and flinging the sindoor powder to look at the strange sight. F.M. shook with fear.

✼✼✼

Freddy wished his big brother were there to help him catch Uday. F.M.'s strength and speed would totally do the trick. But it was up to Freddy alone.

Freddy was pretty mad now, and Uday knew it as he quickly flew down to the first floor. "You and your big monster brother and your silly monkey and your tricky sister are awfully fun to prank! I'm having such a good time, I may just live here forever!" cheered Uday.

Oh no, that would be HORRIBLE, thought Freddy. *I can't believe I was scared of a naughty little imp. He's not so scary, but he is a whole lot of trouble!*

Freddy chased the yaksha into the lab. Uday giggled when Freddy nearly slipped on the orange goo left over from the explosion earlier. Freddy slid around trying to grab at Uday, but the imp just floated out of his grasp. "You'll never catch me, clumsy boy!" he laughed.

Uday hovered right in front of Freddy, grinning. *Why is he waiting for me?* thought Freddy. *Is it a trick?* Freddy ran at Uday again and was just inches away when he caught sight of a big round shape coming at him from the side.

Oh no! It's another of Dad's flotation bubbles! The bubble oozed all around him. *Now I'm trapped in one too! He won,* thought Freddy, shocked. *Now I'm going to float far away too. And no one can stop Uday from pranking my family.*

Uday laughed louder than he ever had before, "Hee hee! Haw haw! HAHAHAAAAAAAA!"

As the bubble started to rise, Freddy started to give up all hope. But then he heard "Freddy! Hold on!" It was his dad, running in to save him. And Riya too, in tiger form!

The moon must be out now, thought Freddy. *Hopefully those tiger powers come in handy against Uday!*

Victor used his newly-finished controller to slow Freddy's bubble down. "It looks like it's working!" he cheered.

But Uday was busy waving magic sparks from his hands, which pushed the bubble higher. *It's science vs. magic, and magic is winning*, worried Freddy.

"Darn, the signal isn't strong enough!" Victor moaned. Shan and Igor ran into the room, trying not to slip on the orange goo on the floor.

"We'll save you Freddy!" shouted Shan.

"Eeep! Eeep!" screeched Igor in support.

"I have a plan!" announced Riya. She jumped on Victor's shoulders. And using her fantastic cat-like balance, she stood on top of Victor and waved Igor over. She had a piece of straw from Freddy's broom in her paw. She instructed Igor, "Climb onto my shoulders and use the straw to pop the bubble!"

Shan looked worried, but Freddy said, "That's brilliant! Come on, Igor!"

The monkey strained and got the straw high enough to poke at the bubble.

Plink!

It bounced off the thick orange skin of the bubble and didn't get through. Igor strained even harder and tried again, but no luck.

As Uday cackled watching this, suddenly, Shan surprised him from behind and threw him in another of the flotation bubbles. He banged on the sides, but was trapped. "Hey, no fair!" he squealed in frustration.

"I won't have mischief-makers in my house!" Shan scolded. Uday was just distracted enough for Victor to use his controller to lower Freddy's bubble quickly on the straw.

POP!

Orange splattered all over Victor, Shan, Riya, Igor, and Freddy. But they couldn't have been happier to be covered in goo.

Now Uday really started to have a hissy fit. "You're spoiling all my fun!" he complained.

"Ah, so you don't like it now that the tables have turned on YOU!" Freddy said triumphantly. "Maybe we can just get that bubble to float him all the way home," said Victor.

Victor quickly worked to tweak his flotation bubble controller.

"If we can boost the signal stronger, it will be no match for Uday's magic!" Freddy pitched in, and they got it working together.

"All right, here it goes." Victor pressed the controller, and the bubble went zooming out of the palace, sending the imp all the way back to where he came from.

He wasn't really that scary after all—and certainly not as scary as a ghost, thought Freddy.

Chapter 10:
The Missing Monster

And with that, the mystery is solved and the mayhem is over!" cheered Freddy. "We four unlikely sleuths worked surprisingly well together to save the day, haven't we?"

"But wait, where's our fourth detective?" wondered Riya.

"Oh wait . . . F.M. got carried away in a bubble too! Where could he be, Dad? You didn't send him away with Uday, did you?!" Freddy cried out.

Victor looked at his controller and was shocked. "No, but there's another bubble landing right now in the town. He's with all the villagers from the festival!"

"Oh no! That's his worst nightmare," worried Freddy.

Victor said, "I can pop it remotely so hopefully he can escape before they see him." And he pushed the button.

***

At that very moment, F.M. was frozen in fear as his bubble hovered over the town. Just as it touched the ground it went *POP!*, splattering F.M. and the crowd in orange from head to toe. F.M. covered his eyes, waiting for people to scream in terror.

But a huge cheer erupted. They thought he was the best Biska Jatra partier of them all! F.M. grimaced and said, "Hi everyone!" And then he ran as fast as his legs could go. He sprinted all the way to the palace, dropping orange glops the whole time.

When F.M. arrived home, he told his terrifying bubble story.

"See? You didn't have a bad experience with humans this time," Riya pointed out.

"Riya's right! People aren't that bad," said Freddy. "But sometimes little brothers can be kind of mean," he continued. "I'm sorry for accusing you of being the prankster, Riya. I know now you would never do such a thing. And thank you for saving me. Otherwise, I'd probably be floating somewhere over China right now."

Shan was thrilled with Freddy's apology. "Thank you for apologizing to your sister, Freddy." He looked at his mom's smile and was happy to make her proud. Then Freddy glanced around the lab and said, "Oh wow, I still have so much cleanup to do." His joy turned to sorrow as he thought about all the chores he had to do that night: clean the lab, clean his room, put away his laundry. . . .

Shan gave him a hug and said, "It's been quite a day. You can start on those chores tomorrow."

"Whew!" sighed Freddy. *That's too many chores for one night*, he thought.

"I know I was disappointed that you went to the festival instead of taking care of your responsibilities," Shan told him. "But by finding our intruder and helping Dad with the controller, you contributed in a BIG way to helping our family and home."

Victor added, "I'm proud of you—and of how brave you were as well."

Shan gave Freddy a hug. "And I owe you an apology too for suspecting you were the prankster. Now, why don't you take Riya to see the very end of the festival?"

"No thanks!" Freddy said to a surprised Shan and Victor. "I've had enough surprises and splatters for one day! I might as well get a *little* head start on cleaning."

And with that Freddy headed up to his room. A shocked Shan and Victor laughed, and F.M. and Riya walked up the staircase to help him.

BUBBLE TROUBLE

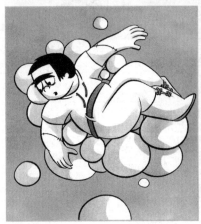

Journey to some magical places and outer space, rock out, and find your inner superhero with these other chapter book series from Little Bee Books!

Tales of
SASHA
#1
The Big
Secret

by Alexa Pearl
illustrated by Paco Sordo

ISLE OF
MISFITS
FIRST CLASS
BOOK 1

by JAMIE MAE   illustrated by FREYA HARTAS

ELLA AND
OWEN
BOOK 1
THE CAVE OF
AAAAAH!
DOOM!

by Jaden Kent   illustrated by Iryna Bodnaruk

Mighty
MEG
BOOK 1
and the Magical Ring

BY
Sammy
Griffin

Illustrated
By
Micah
Player

Read on for a sneak peek from the third book in the MONSTER AND ME **series.**

Chapter 1:
Monsters Attack!

Freddy von Frankenstein stood bold and brave, even though he was surrounded by terrifying monsters. It was the most thrilling and chilling moment of his young life. Fortunately, his big brother and best friend, F.M., was by his side. And his brother was Frankenstein's Monster, perhaps the most powerful monster of all.

The brothers stood back-to-back, ready to take them all on. A creepy mummy wrapped in rotting bandages stumbled toward them. A swamp creature dripping with grimy goop rose out of some ooze. A chupacabra flashed its razor-sharp teeth at them. The magical yaksha, named Uday, that Freddy and

F.M. had defeated weeks ago was there as well. Worse yet, the giant yeti from their first fantastical encounter was also there, roaring with hunger!

"And watch out for that little guy too," Freddy warned, pointing out a tiny man with a red hat and big beard.

"Ha!" laughed Freddy's father, Victor von Frankenstein. "Gnomes aren't scary!"

Freddy's sister, Riya, asked, "What's a gnome?"

"Hey, I'm trying to give a presentation here!" Freddy complained in frustration. "*All* supernatural creatures can be threats!" Freddy pointed at pictures of all the monsters projected on the wall of Victor's laboratory. Victor turned on the lights and turned off the projector.

"Gnomes are friendly little forest creatures, Riya. It seems that Freddy ran out of ideas for scary monsters."

"Well, you get the idea!" Freddy shot back. "Now can I explain my plan?"

Victor sighed and said, "You only have a few

minutes. I'm in the middle of a delicate experiment with my mega-magnetomoter. The magnetic ray charge is almost too big!" Freddy's dad was maybe the smartest scientist in the world. His lab was full of amazing inventions he was always testing out.

Freddy rushed through his speech as fast as he could, "Well, we've already had two monsters show up on the mountain—a yeti and a yaksha."

"And Riya too! She turns into a tiger, after all," added F.M.

"Riya too," Freddy agreed. "That's THREE fantasticals in just a few weeks, which means more are sure to show up! Riya mentioned that something drew her here our mountain. If she's right, then there could be other fantasticals on their way right now! So, I want to create a team as an extra credit project. F.M. and I will go on patrol to find any that wind up here. We're the Supernatural Action Search Squad!"

Freddy eagerly looked at everyone to see what they thought of his idea.

Chapter 2:
The Supernatural Action Search Squad

F.M. got a big grin and jumped up and down, "I love meeting new monsters!" But Riya frowned because it seemed like Freddy thought these "fantasticals" were all trouble. Victor thought for a bit and said, "I know you're a little scared of fantasticals . . ."

Freddy protested, "I'm not scared." F.M. and Riya smiled at each other because they knew Freddy was more afraid than he would admit. Victor continued, "But this doesn't really sound like schoolwork to me. And since I'm in charge of your homeschooling, I don't think this is how you should spend your time. You're always coming up with extra credit projects like this instead of doing your ACTUAL homework."

Freddy pouted and started to protest, but Victor

added, "I'm so busy in my lab these days, I can't always be interrupted with these crazy extra credit plans of yours. I'm beginning to think we should put you in school down in the village."

Oh no! Not regular school down in the town at the bottom of the mountain, thought Freddy. *That wouldn't be fun at all!* Freddy quickly changed the subject back to his plan to avoid THAT idea. "I've got the squad project all figured out though!"

Freddy unveiled the secret handshake to everyone, which was way too complicated. F.M. messed up and laughed at himself. Even Freddy lost track of some of the steps and got frustrated, making Riya giggle. Victor was unimpressed.

"And I've already made special tech for our search," Freddy continued. "Check out our team badges!" Freddy tried to show one off, but the badge zoomed out of his hand, across the room, and clanked onto F.M.'s forehead. F.M. tried to look up at the badge, confused.

Victor laughed, "Oops, guess my magnetic ray charge must be too strong, because that badge attached to the metal plate in his head!" Riya stifled another laugh. This presentation was not going quite how Freddy had hoped.

"So far I'm not seeing anything that involves homework," warned Victor.

"Well, then you're gonna love this!" Freddy boasted. "Check out our upgraded, high tech wrist communicators!"

"So, how is any of this really going to help track fantasticals?" Riya asked.

Freddy rolled his eyes. "I can't believe you don't know the kinds of things that super secret clubs need."

Riya looked confused. "But you just told us about it. How can it be a secret?"

Freddy paused and thought. "Uh, well, because, huh . . . Well here's a wrist communicator of your own!" he said, changing the subject.

Yeah, try it on!" F.M. said. "This one is too small for my wrists."

Riya was dazzled, "Wow, thanks Freddy!"

Freddy, continuing with his presentation, proudly announced, "Finally, best of all, I've built a long-distance motion sensor. If someone shows up on the mountain we can check out if they are a fantastical!"

Victor nodded his head and admitted, "Well an invention like that actually sounds worthy of *some* extra credit. All right, you win. Go test it out. If it works, we can make this an extra credit assignment!"

"YAAAYYY!" shouted Freddy.

"But only if your brother goes with you!" warned Victor. "And I'm serious about you doing all your regular homework too. If you can't keep up with all of it, we might need to put you in a real school."

I'd better get out of here before Dad talks any more about school, thought Freddy. So he quickly pushed F.M. out of the lab. "Gotta go test out my sensor tech!"

he said while running out of the house.

Victor turned to Riya and asked, "Could you please keep an eye on them too? You're the oldest, and with the sun setting your tiger powers and cool head will come in handy."

Riya felt proud that Victor trusted her. She nodded and ran out to follow her new brothers.

Cort Lane is a producer, creative exec, and storyteller with two decades of kids' television experience at Marvel/Disney and Mattel. He has credits on over 50 productions, two Emmy nominations, and two NAACP Image Nominations. He currently serves on GLAAD's Kids and Family Advisory Council, and is working on the new *My Little Pony* series on Netflix.

Ankitha Kini is an animator, comics artist, and illustrator. She loves stories steeped in culture and history. A mix of whimsy, fact, and fantasy brings life to her creature-filled world. When she's not drawing, she likes to travel and to make friends with stray cats. She studied Animation Film Design at NID in Ahmedabad, India, and now lives in Eindhoven, the Netherlands.

ankithakini.com